MW00905888

EXPLORING THE CANADIAN ARCTIC

People of the North

by Heather Kissock
and Audrey Huntley

Weigl

Published by Weigl Educational Publishers Limited
6325 10 Street SE
Calgary, Alberta
T2H 2Z9

www.weigl.com

Library and Archives Canada Cataloguing in Publication data available upon request.
Fax 403-233-7769 for the attention of the Publishing Records department.

ISBN 978-1-55388-958-8 (hard cover)
ISBN 978-1-55388-962-5 (soft cover)

Printed in the United States of America
1 2 3 4 5 6 7 8 9 0 13 12 11 10 09

Project Coordinator: Heather Kissock
Design: Terry Paulhus

All of the Internet URLs given in the book were valid at the time of publication. However, due to the dynamic nature of the Internet,
some addresses may have changed, or sites may have ceased to exist since publication. While the author and publisher regret any
inconvenience this may cause readers, no responsibility for any such changes can be accepted by either the author or the publisher.

Every reasonable effort has been made to trace ownership and to obtain permission to reprint copyright material. The publishers
would be pleased to have any errors or omissions brought to their attention so that they may be corrected in subsequent printings.

Weigl acknowledges Getty Images as its primary image supplier for this title.

We gratefully acknowledge the financial support of the Government of Canada through the Book Publishing Industry Development
Program (BPIDP) for our publishing activities.

Contents

Beyond 60 Degrees

C anada's Arctic region is a vast area that covers more than 40 percent of the country's total land. The Northwest Territories, Yukon, Nunavut, and the northern tip of Quebec make up this area.

Any land in Canada above 60 degrees latitude is considered the North. This imaginary line became the border of the Arctic region when Saskatchewan and Alberta were declared provinces in 1905.

With almost total darkness in the winter and near total sunlight in the summer, Canada's Arctic region is known as the Land of the Midnight Sun. Here, much of the land is permanently frozen, and trees cannot grow. Shrubs, mosses, and lichens are the only plants that can survive the cold climate. Although temperatures may reach more than 20 degrees Celsius in the summer, the season is very short and wet.

Despite its harsh climate, people have lived in Canada's Arctic region for as long as 10,000 years. Today, more than 100,000 people call Canada's North home. In Nunavut, 85 percent of the population is primarily Inuit. In the Northwest Territories, Aboriginal Peoples make up about 50 percent of the population. In the Yukon, an estimated 25 percent of the population is Aboriginal.

Inuit live throughout Canada's northern regions, particularly in Nunavut.

Early Peoples

People have lived in the area now known as the Canadian North for at least 10,000 years. Shortly after the last **Ice Age**, First Nations from southern parts of North America began moving up toward the continent's tree line. The Cree and Dene were among these groups. Many still live in this tree line area today.

The first residents of Canada's **High Arctic** arrived several centuries later. Archaeologists have found evidence that people lived in this area for at least 4,500 years. This is when a group of people known as the pre-Dorset arrived in the area. These people formed small groups to follow the caribou and seal. They used tools and weapons made of flint and bone, and lived in tents made of animal skin.

About 2,500 years ago, the Dorset, or Tuniit, people emerged. In the spring, they hunted walruses, caribou, small mammals, and seals. They caught fish in the summer and trapped seals in the fall and winter. Some of the food they caught was stored in **caches** for the long winter seasons. For about 1,000 years, they were the sole group of people to live in this far north region.

■ Whalebone or driftwood was used to make the frame of an Inuit tent. Sealskin or caribou hides covered the tent frame.

It was at this time that Inuit ancestors called the Thule arrived in what is now Canada's Far North. They travelled hundreds of miles from Alaska and settled in the parts of Canada now known as Nunavut, the Northwest Territories, and northern Quebec. Thule summer homes were tents made of animal skins. Their winter homes were sunk into the ground. They had a stone floor, a whalebone or stone frame, and a roof of seal skin. The Thule hunted for game with bows and arrows or spears. In summer, they hunted for whales from kayaks and fished with spears and hooks.

■ Traditional kayaks were made from driftwood or whalebone and were covered with stretched animal skins. The kayak was waterproofed with whale fat.

Over time, the Thule became known as the Inuit. The Inuit were spread across northern North America. Their lifestyle was based on the migration cycles of various animal herds, including the caribou. As these animals were an important food source, the Inuit followed the herds wherever they went. Many Inuit moved from one place to another during the different seasons.

Traditional Inuit homes were based on the needs of the season. In summer, the Inuit lived in tents made from wood and animal skins. In winter, they lived in houses made from sod, stone, or ice and snow. In some parts of Canada, the Inuit lived in igloos.

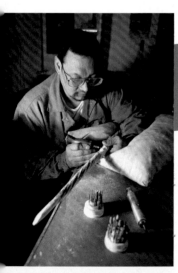

ARCTIC ARTWORK

Archaeologists can learn much about people from the past by studying the **artifacts** they left behind. Some of these artifacts include pieces of art. The Inuit have always used materials from their natural surroundings to create artwork. They carved rock, bones, and ivory to create tools. They also created decorative masks and rock carvings. One mask found near the Hudson Strait in Quebec was carved from ivory. The mask, which depicts a face, is believed to be about 2,000 years old. It is called the Tyara mask, after the name of the site where it was found. Rock carvings, called petroglyphs, have been found in the same region. The carvings, which show faces, were made nearly 1,000 years ago.

Coming North

A s the glaciers of the last Ice Age receded, people began travelling into areas that had once been covered with ice. Some, such as Inuit ancestors, travelled from far away, following animals herds and other food sources. Others, such as Canada's First Nations, expanded the lands that were already theirs. This is how Canada's North came to be inhabited.

LEGEND

10,000 to 5,000 years ago
North America's First Nations move northward to the tree line after the Ice Age.

5,000 to 4,000 years ago
The Tuniit, or Dorset, people arrive from the west and move eastward across what is now Canada's Arctic.

1,000 years ago
The Thule arrive from Alaska, displacing the Tuniit.

U.S.A.

YUKON

NORTHWEST TERRITORIES

BRITISH COLUMBIA

ALBER

SAS

U.S.A.

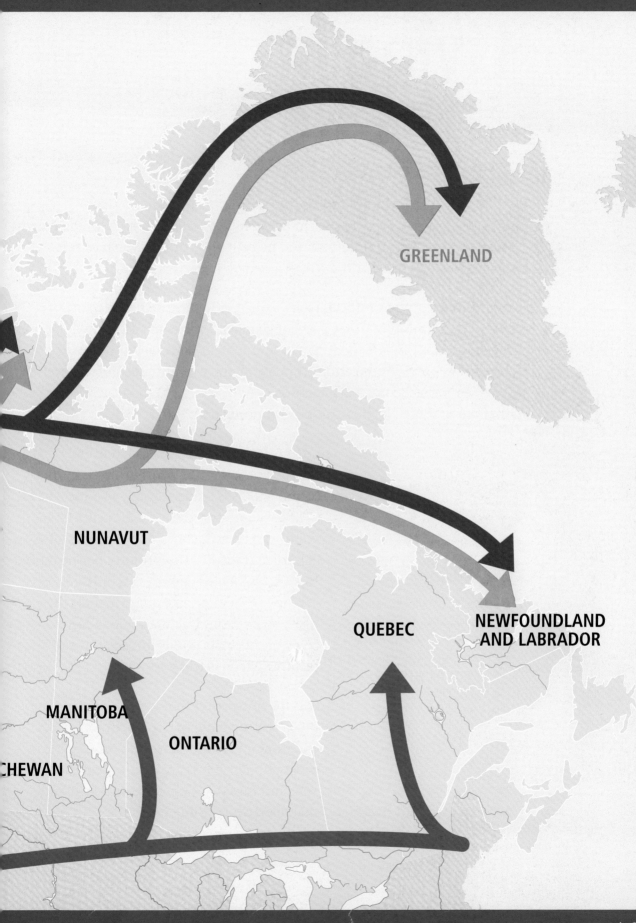

GREENLAND

NUNAVUT

QUEBEC

NEWFOUNDLAND
AND LABRADOR

MANITOBA

ONTARIO

CHEWAN

Living in the North

Canada's North has undergone several major changes since Aboriginal Peoples started living in the area. Today, life in the North is a combination of past and present ways of life. Much of this depends in which part of the North a person lives.

Communities in the southern part of the region have access to many of the conveniences found in other parts of Canada. Cities such as Whitehorse and Yellowknife have movie theatres, shopping malls, and various types of schools that provide education from elementary to post-secondary levels. Many people in the northern territories have moved to these larger centres. Other parts of the North are almost unpopulated.

Judy Wilson

Judy Wilson is the nurse in-charge at the Rosie Ovayuk Health Centre in Tuktoyaktuk—a four-nurse facility in the community of 1,000 people. Born in Fort Churchill, Manitoba, the nurse of 31 years cites the advantages of working in the North.

"The rewards are incredible. The **autonomy** we have there and the ability to be a part of a community is great. I love practicing. I love my job. It's so rare to have a job that you can learn something every day. I'm challenged in every way. It's great from a professional point of view."

Life in Canada's North is much more expensive than in the southern part of the country. This is because many products have to be brought into the area. Transporting goods can be awkward due to the lack of extensive transportation routes. For instance, Iqaluit, Nunavut's capital, can only be reached by boat or airplane. Much of the time, boats cannot be used due to ice coverage. Getting goods into Iqaluit can be quite expensive as a result.

It is for this reason that people living in the more remote parts of the North rely on traditional foods for survival. Among the most popular foods are Arctic char, caribou, seal, and muskox. Other favourites include maktaaq, which is the raw outer skin of the whale, and a dip called misiraq, which is aged seal blubber.

Even the remote areas have acquired many modern conveniences. Permanent houses have replaced the igloos and tents that northern Aboriginal Peoples once used for shelter. Snowmobiles are used to travel from place to place instead of dogsleds. Even though the region is physically isolated, it is linked to the rest of the planet through technology. Satellites beam communications signals from Iqaluit to locations around the world. More and more, young people are taking advantage of technology, including the Internet. Through the Internet, people in the North can order wool from New Zealand, watch a Brazilian soccer match, or even chat with people in Tokyo.

■ Located on the shores of Great Slave Lake, Yellowknife is a bustling city of 20,000 people.

■ Northern Aboriginal Peoples use snowmobiles for hunting and to transport goods from one community to another.

THE PEOPLE OF THE ARCTIC

ARCTIC COMMUNITIES
What is it like to live in such a cold place where the land is covered with ice and snow, and there are a few hours of daylight during the winter?

There are many small communities in the Arctic region of Canada. Here are the names of some of the places - Arviat, Cambridge Bay, Cape Dorset, Rankin Inlet, Pond Inlet, Pangnirtung,and Iqaluit .

Rankin Inlet - photo
Cape Dorset - photo

Some towns have hospitals, police, schools, fire departments, stores, and churches . Power generating stations provide electricity. Communities get water delivered by trucks and the sewage is also taken away by trucks. Homes have a tank to hold the water. Pipes (running above the ground) provide some homes with water and take away the sewage.

During the winter, blizzards are caused by the winds. On stormy days, people can lose their way because of the blowing snow.

In the winter there are alot of things to do - hockey, sliding, skating, sledding, snowboarding, skiing, curling, and playing in the snow.

In the summer, there are twenty hours of sunlight, and the sky is never totally dark.

THE PEOPLE
Many groups of people live in the Arctic. Some groups have lived there for thousands of years.

Business in the North

In the past, the daily work of northern Aboriginal Peoples revolved around activities that helped them live in their environment. Men went hunting and fishing for food. Women made clothing, cared for the children, and prepared food when the men returned from the hunt. To do their work, men and women used tools, such as knives and combs, that had been carved from animal bones. The focus of their activities changed, however, as people began arriving from other parts of the country, bringing with them a different way of life. The commercial potential of the North and its resources began to change the way the area's Aboriginal Peoples lived their lives. Earning money became the new way to survive.

■ Tourists from all over the world venture to the Yukon's Ivvavik National Park to view the unspoiled wilderness of the Arctic tundra.

Inuit carvings that were used as tools developed into works of art as newcomers to the area expressed an interest in purchasing these unique creations. Over time, creating art became a business. **Co-operatives** were formed to help the Inuit sell their art within Canada and other parts of the world. As a result, a growing part of the Arctic economy was based on exporting Inuit art. Today, a large number of Inuit residents earn extra money by creating and selling their artwork.

One of the main reasons people are moving to the North is because of the wealth of natural resources in the area. Diamonds and gold are just some of the minerals that can be found in abundance north of 60 degrees. The area is also rich in oil and natural gas. Mines and drilling sites are scattered across the North and its surrounding waters. Workers at these job sites are a combination of non-residents and Aboriginal Peoples.

With this influx of non-resident workers comes the need for services to support them. These services include health care, education, and government. Many Aboriginal Peoples have found work in these areas. In fact, the **treaty** that made Nunavut a territory states that 85 percent of government workers must be Inuit.

Tourism is rapidly becoming a major industry in the Canadian North. People are travelling to the area to view the unspoiled scenery and unique wildlife. Outfitting and guiding companies, along with visitor centres, museums, and parks provide residents with jobs throughout the year. Many of these organizations rely on the knowledge of the area's Aboriginal Peoples.

INUIT SCULPTURE

The Inuit are well known for their sculptures. Inuit artists get their inspiration from their surrounding, history, and culture. Their sculptures often depict people or animals. Most Inuit sculptures are made from stone found in the Arctic region. Bones and ivory are also used. Different types of stone are used depending on the region where the artists live. Soapstone and serpentine are most commonly used. Serpentine comes in a variety of colours, including black, brown, and green. Inuit artists also use quartz and marble in their sculptures.

Changing Ways

The arrival of industries such as mining and oil drilling have had a major impact on the North and the people that live there. Having natural resources that are wanted worldwide has done much to improve the economy of the area. However, the development of these industries has taken place on the traditional lands of the North's Aboriginal Peoples. As a result, the lands are being repurposed in ways that are affecting traditional Aboriginal ways of life. To compensate for this change, the region's Aboriginal Peoples have negotiated land claims with the federal government. These claims provide Aboriginal Peoples with a variety of benefits, ranging from project funding to control over parts of the land and how it will be used.

One of the best-known land claims was finalized in 1999, with the development of Nunavut. The area that Nunavut now covers has long been inhabited mostly by Inuit. The territory was created specifically to provide the Inuit with control over their land. With oil and mineral finds in the region, the land claim was designed to ensure that the Inuit had a voice in the effects development would have on their lives. When finalized, the land claim gave the Inuit control over 351,000 square kilometres of land. It also gave the Inuit mining rights in certain areas, hunting and fishing rights, and payment of about $1.15 billion to the Nunavut Trust over a period of 14 years. The trust is in charge of protecting and building on this money to ensure that Nunavut remains a thriving territory for years to come. Other Aboriginal groups have made similar agreements with the federal government, but the Nunavut land claim remains the largest in Canadian history.

First-hand Account

Zach Kunuk

Zach Kunuk is a filmmaker. His Inuktitut-language film *Atanarjuat* (*The Fast Runner*) won the 2001 best first film award at the Cannes Film Festival. *Atanarjuat* is Canada's first feature-length fiction film written, produced, directed, and acted by Inuit.

"I think Inuit people are speaking out more since we got the land claim and we got our own territory. I think Inuit gained confidence in our culture."

Even with these types of controls in place in the North, the land and way of life continue to change as more outside influences arrive in the area. Many Aboriginal Peoples are concerned that their languages and traditions will gradually disappear as they become more and more **assimilated** into mainstream Canadian life.

Nunavut's flag was unveiled when the area officially became a territory. It features an inukshuk, which is a rock sculpture the Inuit made to guide travellers across the Arctic.

Nunavut's territorial government building is located in Iqaluit.

ening to Our Past

tudent log in | Instructor log in | Your Personal Page

the Creation of Nunavut

ey into Inuit Traditional
dge
of Change
meets South
opment of Government
es in the Arctic
Creation of Nunavut
hanging the Face of Canada

The Creation of Nunavut

Summary:

This section presents the life stories of Inuit leaders who played an essential role in the long political process that led to the creation of Nunavut. This defining moment of Canadian history is here told by the very actors who invested their lives in making Nunavut come to life.

In the Inuit Tapirisat Canada document, *Proposed Agreement in Principle for Northwest Territories Land Claims*, the creation of Nunavut was set as a prime negotiating principle. The protection of Inuit language and culture was also set as a high priority. The document listed principles over which the parties should reach agreement. When John Amagoalik introduced this document to the new DIAND Minister, Hugh Faulkner, in December 1977 in Iqaluit, John said, "The 1976 proposal was a lawyer's agreement; this one is from the people."

At its Annual General Meeting in Igloolik in September 1979, the Inuit Land Claims Commission, chaired by John Amagoalik, presented a discussion paper called *Political Development in Nunavut* that explained in more detail the position of the Inuit negotiating team.

That same year, Peter Ittinuar was elected to Parliament for the riding of Nunatsiaq as a New Democratic Party member. He was the first native Canadian ever elected to Parliament with the exception of Louis Riel who was elected in 1874, while still in hiding in the United States. With Ittinuar, Inuit gained another important national stage where they could discuss publicly their dream of a new territory.

supported by a majority of aboriginal and Inuit MLAs at the Yellowknife Legislati the Northwest Territories to decide on the question of dividi supported division.

A Language to Keep

As more and more work opportunities become available in the North, the region is seeing an influx of people from other parts of the country. These people are bringing their cultural influences with them. While this is exposing the Inuit and other Aboriginal groups to new ways of life, there is concern that their traditional ways are in jeopardy. One area that is of special concern is the traditional languages of northern peoples. Many of the people coming to the North speak either French or English. In order to communicate with these newcomers, Aboriginal Peoples are acquiring these new languages. There is a fear that, over time, French and English will replace the traditional northern languages.

Today, Inuit children are exposed to English at an early age. To keep Inuktitut alive, efforts are being made to teach the language at all school levels.

Steps are being taken to ensure that traditional languages survive this transition. Much of this effort is being put into teaching the language to younger generations. The Pigiarvik program has been developed to preserve, protect, and promote the Inuktitut language among young Inuit. This is being done in a variety of ways. One of the most important steps is the interviewing of Inuit elders. These interviews pass the language along to younger generations and transfer traditional Inuit knowledge and stories so that the Inuit way of life is retained. Much of the information from these interviews is being digitized through websites, CDs, and other technology to ensure its longevity. Finally, a series of magazines is being developed for northern classrooms that relay Inuit traditions to Inuit children in the Inuktitut language.

Efforts are being made to keep the language relevant in other ways. Plans are already under way to create the Inuit Knowledge Centre. The centre will focus on research by Inuit academics. Plans are also underway to develop the Inuit Language Development Institute, which will work to preserve Inuktitut and revitalize it among the Inuit people. Like the Pigiarvik program, the institute will gather language and story samples from Inuit elders. It will also develop instruction materials and provide training for teaching the Inuktitut language.

A WRITTEN LANGUAGE

Inuktituk is an **oral** language, meaning that it is communicated only through speech. It is spoken in many different **dialects**, depending on the northern region where it is used. Until the arrival of Europeans, the Inuit did not have a written language. They communicated orally and through carvings and art. European **missionaries** taught the Inuit a form af writing called syllabics. This is a system of writing that uses symbols to represent letters and sounds. Syllabics are found on signs and other written forms of communication throughout the North.

A Different Landscape

While the arrival of more people to the Arctic is having an effect on language, the industries these people work in are having a huge effect on the land. Aboriginal Peoples all over Canada have a strong connection to the land. This is especially apparent in the North, where many still live by the traditions of their **ancestors**. The land development required to create industry is affecting the air, environment, animals, and plants that live within the region. All of this has a direct impact on the area's Aboriginal Peoples.

Roads and pipelines are being built across caribou **migration** paths. The construction is uprooting lichens and plants. This is affecting the amount of food available to caribou, which feed primarily on lichens. Some caribou are not receiving the nutrients they require as a result, causing a reduction in the number of calves born each year. This, in turn, affects the ability of Aboriginal Peoples to hunt enough caribou to eat.

Construction projects associated with industry, along with industry itself, create pollution. Toxic chemicals are being put into the air, water, and soil. This affects every living thing in the food chain because plants absorb the toxins, animals eat the plants, and humans eat the animals. Land that was once a great resource to Aboriginal Peoples is becoming a threat to their way of life.

GLOBAL WARMING

Industry is just one factor in the changing Arctic environment. Global warming also affects the plants and animals that Aboriginal Peoples depend on. The warmer temperatures are changing animal and plant behaviour. Plants are blooming at different times, which is causing problems for the migration cycles of certain animals, including caribou. Caribou have followed a specific cycle for thousands of years. It is meant to get them to their calving grounds when plants are blooming so that there is plenty of food for them and their young. Now, plants are blooming earlier, and the caribou are missing the peak season. This is causing a decline in births and a lower survival rate for newborn calves.

Caribou are a main food source for many northern Aboriginal Peoples. Changing migration patterns and decreasing populations are causing problems for Aboriginal hunters.

Many caribou are reluctant to cross roads. They often change their migration path to avoid high-use road systems.

Discarded oil barrels can leak toxins into the ground.

Due to the growing oil industry, more pipelines are being built in the North. Some are encroaching on wildlife sanctuaries that were created to provide a safe place for birds, polar bears, caribou, and other animals to live.

A Way of Life

Northern Aboriginal Peoples have long been influenced by people from other lands. Early explorers from Europe introduced them to new foods, languages, and ways of life. Today, many of the influences coming to the North are based on new technologies.

Umiaks were used to transport people to hunting grounds in the summer. They could hold up to 20 people.

THEN	NOW
LANGUAGE	
The Inuit had a unique language called Inuktitut. It was an oral language that contained words directly related to their way of life.	Inuktitut now contains versions of English words. The Inuit first began using these words when European explorers arrived in the area and introduced them to items such as sugar and paper. "*Sukaq*" and "*paipaaq*" became the words the Inuit used to identify these items.
RELIGION	
Traditional Inuit religion is rooted in nature and spirituality. They believed that plants, animals, people, and natural landmarks had a spirit that should be honoured.	Many Inuit are Christians. They follow a religion that originated in the Middle East and was brought to Canada by missionaries.
HOUSING	
In summer, northern Aboriginal Peoples lived in tents, teepees, or wooden lodges. The Inuit built igloos for winter living. All housing was designed for ease of movement. Shelters could be put up and taken down quickly as the people followed animal herds.	Northern Aboriginal Peoples live in permanent housing throughout the year. They still use tents and igloos when they go on hunting trips.
WINTER TRAVEL	
Dogsleds were used to travel to hunting sites.	Many Aboriginal Peoples use snowmobiles when hunting.
WATER TRAVEL	
Umiaks and kayaks were used for fishing trips.	Many Aboriginal Peoples use motorboats for water travel.

Industrial Development

One of the first oil discoveries in the North took place at Norman Wells, in the Northwest Territories. The wells remain active today.

AT ISSUE

The demand for oil, gas, and other natural resources is causing companies to look for new sources. In doing so, they often find the resources in places that have been relatively untouched by development, such as Canada's North. When companies begin to move into new areas, they bring change with them. Deciding if this change is positive or negative for the region can be difficult.

Developing the North's resources can do much to improve the region's economy. Money comes into the area via the sale of these resources, as well as through the people that come to work in the area. These people bring with them new ideas and ways of doing things.

Development, however, comes at a cost. Roads, pipelines, and other construction projects damage and pollute the land and air. This affects the animals and plants that live there, and in turn, the people that rely on them. As well, the cultural influences of the area's newcomers impact on the traditional life of the region's Aboriginal Peoples.

Industrial development has the potential to upset the natural balance of the North. This raises the issue of whether Arctic development can or should continue.

Should development continue in the Arctic?

A debate occurs when people research opposing viewpoints on an issue and argue them following a special format and rules. Debating is a useful skill that helps people express their opinions on specific subjects.

1. Decide how you feel about the issue described.
2. Ask a friend to argue the opposing viewpoint.
3. Use the information in this book and other sources to prepare a two-minute statement about your viewpoint.
4. Present your argument, and listen while a friend gives his or her argument. Make notes, and prepare a response.
5. Present your rebuttal and a final statement. Let your friend do the same. Did your friend's arguments change how you feel about the issue?

Arctic Peoples

Canada's North is home to a range of Aboriginal Peoples, including First Nations, Inuit, and Métis. Some live in large centres, while others live in isolated areas. What unites all northern peoples is the challenge of living in the extreme Arctic environment.

INUIT	MÉTIS	GWICH'IN
The Inuit live across the northern Arctic, from Alaska to Greenland. They have up to 20 different dialects of Inuktitut. Which dialect is used depends mainly on where they live in the Arctic. Even with this broad range in the language, Inuit from different areas can usually understand each other.	Métis can trace their ancestry back to the fur trade, when Aboriginal women married European men. The Métis that live in the North are **descendants** of the Dene and European fur traders. Many Métis speak a language called Michif, which combines French and Aboriginal words.	The Gwich'in live along the Crow River in the Yukon. Their traditional lands covered 26,000 square kilometres. The Gwich'in were hunter-gatherers, meaning that they hunted animals for food as well as gathered plants. They continue to depend on caribou as their major food source.

Canada's North is a unique setting, a place where the ways of the past mingle with present influences. The people of northern Canada work hard to maintain their traditional ways. As a result, they contribute much to the cultural landscape of the North and Canada itself.

DENE

The Dene are the largest **First Nation** living in the North. Their traditional lands range from Alaska to the northern Prairies. The Dene are made up of five groups—Dogrib, Slavey, Densuline, Yellowknife, and Sahtu Dene. The Dene were the first peoples to live in the North after the last Ice Age.

TLINGIT

Originally from the Alaska area, the Tlingit moved east to the Yukon in the 1800s. Over time, they also moved into northern British Columbia. The Tlingit have a language by the same name. Very few Tlingit speak it actively, but efforts are underway to have it spoken more in everyday use.

NORTHERN TUTCHONE

The Northern Tutchone live mainly in central Yukon. They are part of a larger group called Tutchone and are connected to the Southern Tutchone. The two groups have very different dialects and have difficulty understanding each other. Traditionally, the Tutchone expressed themselves through song, dance, and storytelling.

Where They Live

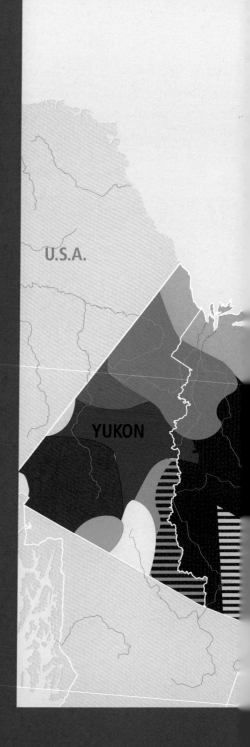

More than 100,000 people live in Canada's North today. They are spread over 75 communities, 55 of which have fewer than 1,000 residents. Even the two largest cities, Yellowknife and Whitehorse, have only about 20,000 and 25,600 inhabitants respectively.

Yukon is home to eight First Nations language groups. Seven of these groups belong to the Athapaskan language group. They are the Gwich'in, Tagish, Kaska, Upper Tanana, Northern Tutchone, Southern Tutchone, and Han. The eighth group is Tlingit.

Inuit people are scattered throughout the North. They number about 45,000 and live in 53 communities in Nunatsiavut (Labrador), Nunavik (Quebec), Nunavut, and the Inuvialuit Settlement Region of the Northwest Territories.

North of 60 degrees, the Métis and Dene are found mainly in the Northwest Territories. Most Dene live in the area around Great Slave Lake. Together, Métis and Dene people make up more than one-third of the population of the Northwest Territories.

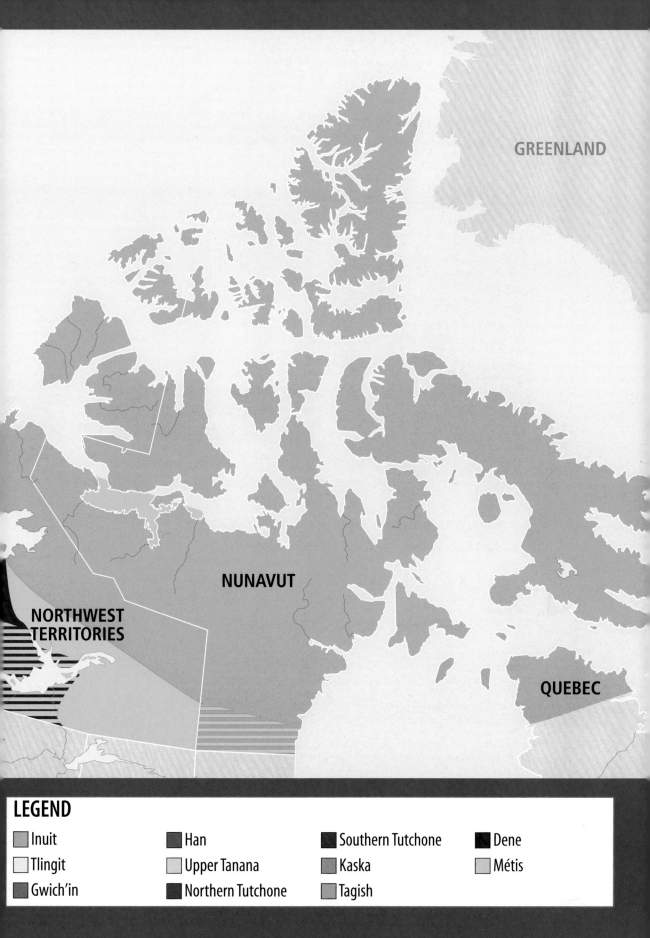

GREENLAND

NUNAVUT

NORTHWEST
TERRITORIES

QUEBEC

LEGEND

Inuit	Han	Southern Tutchone	Dene
Tlingit	Upper Tanana	Kaska	Métis
Gwich'in	Northern Tutchone	Tagish	

Quiz

What have you learned about the northern peoples?
Take this quiz to find out.

1 | Who were the Thule?

2 | What is the capital of Nunavut?

3 | Name four natural resources found in the North that have value all over the world.

4 | How have northern Aboriginal Peoples been compensated for the development of industry on their traditional lands?

5 | What language do Inuit speak?

6 What are three steps the Pigiarvik program will implement to save the Inuit language?

7 What vehicles did the Inuit use in the past?

8 Name three Aboriginal groups that live in Canada's North.

9 How many First Nations language groups are there in the Yukon?

10 Which Aboriginal group speaks Michif?

Answers:
1. Ancestors of today's Inuit
2. Iqaluit
3. Gold, diamonds, gas, oil
4. Through land claims
5. Inuktitut
6. Elder interviews, digitization of traditional knowledge, magazines in Inuktitut for children
7. Kayaks, umiaks, dogsleds
8. Inuit, Métis, Gwich'in, Dene, Tutchone, Tlingit
9. 8
10. Métis

Speaking Inuktitut

The Inuktitut alphabet was created by missionaries long ago. Today, it is still used to communicate the language in a written format. It can also be used to teach the language to people with different language backgrounds.

In Inuktitut, words are formed by combining syllables of the alphabet. Below is a pronunciation chart to help you begin speaking Inuktitut. Use the pronunciation chart to try saying the words in the box called "A Few Words."

Pronunciation

Syllable	Sound
u	oo
au	oh
ai	a (as in "hay")
s	s
ss	ts

A Few Words

English	Inuktitut
Hello	Ai
Goodbye	Assunai
Yes	Aa
No	Auka
Look!	Takugit!
Again	Atiilu

Further Research

Many books and websites provide information on the people of Canada's Arctic. To learn more about these people, borrow books from the library, or surf the Internet.

Most libraries have computers that connect to a database for researching information. If you input a key word, you will be provided with a list of books in the library that contain information on that topic. Nonfiction books are arranged numerically, using their call number. Fiction books are organized alphabetically by the author's last name.

Books

Banting, Erinn. *Inuit* (Canadian Aboriginal Art and Culture series). Calgary: Weigl Educational Publishers Limited, 2008.

Koopmans, Carol. *Denesuline* (Canadian Aboriginal Art and Culture series). Calgary: Weigl Educational Publishers Limited, 2008.

Parker, Janice. *Yukon* (Provinces and Territories of Canada series). Weigl Educational Publishers Limited, 2010.

Websites

To find out more about Canada's North, visit
www.ecokids.ca/pub/eco_info/topics/canadas_north/index.cfm.

For more information on the languages of the Yukon's Aboriginal Peoples, go to
www.gov.yk.ca/aboutyukon/language.html.

Learn more about the traditional ways of the Inuit by visiting
www.collectionscanada.gc.ca/settlement/kids/
021013-2071-e.html.

Glossary

ancestors: relatives who lived a very long time ago

artifacts: items, such as tools, made by humans

assimilated: the process of absorbing one cultural group into another

autonomy: independence

caches: places to store provisions

co-operatives: business organizations owned and operated by a group of people for their mutual benefit

descendants: the offspring of ancestors

dialects: variations of a language that is spoken in a certain place

First Nation: a member of Canada's Aboriginal community who is not Inuit or Métis

High Arctic: the most northerly part of the tundra

Ice Age: a period in which a large part of Earth was covered in ice

migration: to move from one place to another with the change of seasons

missionaries: people who teach others about Christianity

oral: spoken

treaty: an agreement between two or more parties

Index